Renfroe's Christmas

Robert Burch

Renfroe's Christmas

Illustrated by Rocco Negri

The Viking Press   New York

For Annis Duff
with real love

Contents

Renfroe's
Christmas

Carols
to the Cows

"And the third Wise Man fell over backward," said D. J.

"How come?" asked Nutty, who was helping his friend stack cordwood.

"On account of his trick knee acted up just as he started to kneel at the fake manger. And the candle he'd been holding dropped out of his hands and onto the hay right at Baby Jesus's feet."

Renfroe, perched on the chopping block as if he were boss of the woodpile, explained: "Only it wasn't really Baby Jesus."

"Aw, Renfroe!" said D. J. "Nutty knows it wasn't really Baby Jesus."

"Well, I didn't know," said Renfroe, not liking to be spoken down to by his older brother. "I didn't know how much Bible training Nutty might have had." "Bible training" was a term he had picked up from Clara May, his and D. J.'s sister.

"I wish I'd been here to see it," said Nutty, laughing at the account D.J. had given him of last year's program at the church near the crossroads. Nutty had lived with his grandparents at a neighboring farm ever since his mother and father had been killed in a train wreck three years ago. But at Christmas he had always gone to visit relatives down in Savannah. He was fourteen, the same as D. J., and the two of them had been fast friends for so long that it didn't seem possible this would be the first year he had spent the holiday season here in northern Georgia.

"You'll like Christmas hereabouts," said Renfroe. "We have a good time."

Just then Clara May came across the back yard with the milking buckets, and Renfroe, his mind still on Christmas, followed her to the barn. "I expect I'll get lots of presents this year," he told her.

"Getting presents is not the chief joy of the holidays," said Clara May. If D. J. had been along he probably would have told her she was putting on airs, using expressions such as "chief joy of the holidays," but Renfroe liked different ways of saying things. And since Clara May was in the eleventh grade and had been going to school eight years longer than he had, Renfroe "borrowed" words from her whenever he could.

"Then what is one of the . . . chief joys?" he asked.

"Well, gift giving is a special pleasure," she answered. Then she added, quoting from the Bible, "It is more blessed to give than to receive."

Zinnia and June Bug, the two cows, were waiting at

the pasture gate, and Clara May turned them into the lot. They walked into the barn and went directly to their own stable. Renfroe crawled onto the partition that separated it from the rest of the barn, his usual roost whenever he visited with Clara May during milking time. Effie, one of the mules, strolled into the main hall of the barn and over to the partition. She put her head out to be patted while Renfroe went on talking with Clara May.

"Well, I believe I like getting presents best," he said, "no matter what's more blessed."

Clara May, untying a bundle of fodder she had brought from the feed room, looked up and smiled. "I've noticed you've become a bit selfish lately."

He did not care to talk about it, so he asked, "Is that trough a manger?"

"Yes, it is," she said, standing back a step and looking at the wooden box where she had put the cows' feed. "And whenever I hear the Christmas story I can almost see it happening right here in this stable." Then she got back to what Renfroe had wanted to skip over. "Selfishness is something you can make up your mind to overcome," she told him.

He acted as if he had not heard, pretending to be so busy patting Effie that he didn't really have time to do any more talking. But he frowned as he remembered that recently his mother had said she hoped he was not developing a selfish streak. It had been because he hadn't wanted to share with anyone the big bag of parched peanuts his Sunday School teacher had given him. But he didn't want to think about it now, and after a few more minutes with Effie he said to Clara May, "Let's start the cows on carols."

Their father had once read a piece in *Farm Life* magazine about a dairy where phonograph records were played while the milking was being done. It was an experiment to see if music would make the cows so happy they would give extra milk. Since then Clara May sometimes tried singing to the family cows.

Renfroe joined her when he didn't have anything more interesting to do, and they would sing duets. They judged which songs had been the most pleasing to the animals by the amount of milk the cows gave. It was all very scientific, Clara May insisted, and they had discovered that June Bug preferred lively songs such as "Row, Row Your Boat" and "The Bulldog on the Bank," while Zinnia liked slow, sad ones. The most milk she had ever given was the time she listened to them sing "The Dying Cowboy."

"That's a merry idea," said Clara May in answer to Renfroe's suggestion. "Lead off on 'Jingle Bells.' June Bug should like it."

Renfroe sang the verse, and Clara May joined in on the chorus, and they practiced it over and over until June Bug had been milked. Then they switched to "Hark! The Herald Angels Sing" and "O Come, All Ye Faithful" for Zinnia.

They were humming the carols when they went back to the house, and Mrs. Madison said, "With Christmas on our mind, maybe tonight would be a good time to get out the decorations."

"Oh, yes!" said Renfroe, favoring anything that had to do with Christmas. "Tonight would be just exactly a good time."

After supper the big box was brought in from the hall closet, and the decorations were carefully dusted off. Some of the fragile ones had been broken during the year, and these were put aside to be thrown away.

Mrs. Madison held up the angel that had been fastened to the top of the tree in past years. She was made of cloth, stuffed lightly with cotton, and had wool yarn for hair. Features had been drawn on her face with indelible ink, but now all were faded except the eyes; they were still big and bold. Her wings had once been starched to hold them out as if she were flying through the air, but they were limp now, and she looked more like a rag doll than an angel suitable for a treetop. Mr. Madison smiled when his wife held her up. "Poor ol' girl!" he said. "I thought maybe she would fly away before another Christmas!"

D. J. took the angel and held her as if she were a paper airplane. He tried sailing her toward the ceiling, but she landed on the floor with a flop.

"Don't do that!" said Renfroe, going after her.

Clara May left the room and a moment later returned, holding one hand behind her. "I had thought I'd wait another day or two, but I'll bring it out now," she said. At that she held out a new angel. "To the family from me! I made it in Home Ec. class."

"It's lovely," said Mrs. Madison. "How'd you get the wings to curve around so pretty?"

"There's wire in them," said Clara May, and she went

on to explain how the teacher had helped all the students make Christmas decorations.

Mrs. Madison put the new angel with the ornaments that were to be kept. "Could I have the old one if she's not going onto the tree?" Renfroe asked. His mother handed her to him.

"Don't tell us you're gonna take to playing dolls!" said D. J.

"She's not a doll!" said Renfroe. "She's a Christmas angel, and I'll find a place for her outside." And the next afternoon he caught Nutty, when he came over to visit, and persuaded him to help lift the ladder from the wagon shelter out into the back yard. Nutty drove a nail into the smokehouse door almost at the top, and together they fastened the angel to it.

After they returned the ladder to its place, Nutty went into the house to find D. J., but Renfroe stayed outdoors to admire the angel—who seemed to be admiring him. At least, when he would look at her from one direction she appeared to be looking back at him. From a different direction she seemed to be looking out over the back yard—or the whole world.

Andrew Jackson, a black-and-tan hound and the only pet of the Madison household, crawled slowly out from under the porch. "Look at the angel on the smokehouse door!" said Renfroe, and Andrew Jackson turned his head as if he understood. Then he wagged his tail once, which was all he ever wagged it, and walked off toward the barn. "I knew you'd be tickled over it," said Renfroe.

The Angel
on the
Smokehouse
Door

Renfroe strolled around town, looking in shop windows that were decked out for the holidays, and then went back to the hardware store. Maybe his father had finished trading out the ham by now.

Mr. Madison was noted for the smoking process he used to give a special flavor to cured meat, and his country hams were always in demand by townspeople. Today he had brought one to Mr. Peabody at the hardware store. The rest of the family had come along too, but they each had secret things to do at stores up and down the street.

"Christmas is a week from tomorrow," said Mrs. Al Gibbons, who was coming out of Peabody's Store just as Renfroe started into it, "and I'm wondering if I could call on you to be on the program." She lived in the same part of the county as the Madisons and was in charge of the pageant at the church this year.

"Yes, ma'am," said Renfroe. "You could call on me."

"After the pageant," continued Mrs. Gibbons, "we're to have a party, with refreshments and entertainment. I thought perhaps you could do one of your imitations. I've heard that you're good at them."

"Well, thank you," said Renfroe. "What are the refreshments going to be?"

Mrs. Gibbons smiled. "Cake, of course, and ambrosia if we can find fresh coconuts."

"Good!" exclaimed Renfroe. Ambrosia, a dessert made of orange slices and coconut, was one of his favorites.

"But what about your part on the program?" asked Mrs. Gibbons.

"I used to do imitations all the time," said Renfroe, "but that was before I learned how to read. Would you happen to need any of that done at the party?" Before she could answer, he added, "Of course, I don't always recognize big words, but Clara May does, and she'd help me practice if you'd care to pick me out a reading piece."

"Maybe next Christmas," said Mrs. Gibbons. "But for this year won't you think of an imitation—a nice lively one that could be enjoyed by old folks as well as young?"

"Yes, ma'am," promised Renfroe. "I'll try to think you up a number."

"And would you tell Clara May and D. J. that I want them to have parts in the pageant itself," said Mrs. Gibbons, starting away. "But I'll talk to them about it at Sunday School tomorrow."

"I'll be sure and tell them," said Renfroe, and he went ahead to the back of the store.

His father was through shopping, and Mr. Peabody

19

was adding a column of figures on a paper sack. When he finished he looked up. "I owe you seventy-five cents more," he said. "How about a nice pocketknife for young Renfroe there? I've got some real bargains."

"Young Renfroe's mother would sell *me* at a bargain if I were to spend seventy-five cents on a knife for a boy who's already got one."

Renfroe spoke up. "But one blade's broken."

"However, if we didn't go out of our way to tell her," said his father, "and if seventy-five cents would get us two knives, then I'd consider it."

"They come in all prices," said Mr. Peabody, "from a dime to a dollar." He tapped the glass case near the cash register.

Mr. Madison said to Renfroe, "Do you think you could trade out the seventy-five cents on a knife for you and one for D. J. while I go up to the dry-goods store?"

"Yes, sir," said Renfroe, stepping over to the display case.

Mr. Madison gathered up his purchases and left, and Mr. Peabody stood across the counter from Renfroe. "This one costs thirty-five cents," he said. "You could buy two like it and have a nickel left over." He held up a knife with a handle made of horn, but to Renfroe the finest knife in the case was a small one with a white handle. He was almost afraid to ask its price, feeling certain it was a dollar one. Mr. Peabody held it up next, as if he could tell which one Renfroe was thinking about. "Fifty cents," he said, "and ain't it a beauty? The handle is genuine mother-of-pearl."

"Could I hold it?" Renfroe asked, and the storekeeper handed it across to him. Both sides of the handle were perfect, and the blades opened and closed with no trouble at all.

Mr. Peabody took a bigger, wooden-handled knife from the case. "Here's a nice sturdy one," he said, "and it's only a quarter."

Renfroe looked up, thinking at once that he could buy it for D. J. and the mother-of-pearl one for himself. That would be spending twice as much on himself as on D. J., he knew—but still, the little knife with the white handle was exactly what he wanted. Also, he told himself, D. J. just might rather have a wooden-handled one anyway. So he traded for the two knives and walked out to the wagon to wait for the rest of the family.

He patted Andrew Jackson, who always went anywhere the wagon went but refused to get out until he was home again. When D. J. came along, Renfroe held out the twenty-five-cent knife. "It's for you," he said. "But Pa don't want us to tell Mamma on account of sometimes ladies don't understand how it is with boys and knives."

D. J. grinned. "Did he buy you one too?"

"Well, yes," said Renfroe, trying to sound as if he weren't especially pleased about it. "I got a little one." He was glad his mother and Clara May arrived just then and D. J. didn't see that the little knife had a genuine mother-of-pearl handle. And that was all that was said about the unexpected gifts, except that Renfroe did hear D. J. thank his father while they were untying the mules.

On the way home everyone else talked about the

Christmas stock they had seen in stores and friends they'd met. Sitting in the back, Renfroe began to worry: *What if D. J. had been buying the knives? Would he have bought himself one twice as nice as his brother's?* It had not bothered Renfroe a whole lot when Mrs. Madison and Clara May had pointed out that too often he thought of himself first; mothers and sisters were all the time pointing out things. But now he guessed they had been right—down deep he knew it for sure—and maybe he ought to do something about that selfish streak. On the other hand, maybe he wouldn't worry about it. That was it, he would think about something else instead. So he started trying to think of an imitation to do at the Christmas party.

He had spent one summer making up and performing imitations for anyone who would listen. He even did them whether anyone listened or not, explaining them first in a long and roundabout way. But after he had started to school he became so excited about all the interesting things he learned there that in recent years he hadn't thought much about imitations. All the same he guessed he could come up with a new one even if he was out of practice, and he began working on one in his mind.

At home after supper he decided to try it out. The family sat around the open fire in the front room, D. J. popping corn and Clara May and Mrs. Madison stringing it into Christmas-tree garlands—all that wasn't mixed with salt and butter for everyone to eat hot.

"Well, here it is," said Renfroe, after persuading D. J.

to hold off on another batch of corn so the popping noises wouldn't interfere with his act: "It's going to be Mr. Fringe Martin singing 'Joy to the World' at last year's Christmas program when all of a sudden the third Wise Man accidentally drops his candle in the hay and Mrs. Eli Arnold screams on account of it's her baby in the same manger as the hay but she won't scream long because Mr. Eli is the first Wise Man and he snatches up the baby and yells 'I got him!' while Mr. Otis Conway, the second Wise Man, shucks off his cloak and snuffs out the fire as pretty as you please but then forgets he's only Mr. Otis Conway instead of the real second Wise Man because he says to everybody, 'We've had a little commotion here in Bethlehem, but if you'll all sit back down we'll get on with things,' and everybody sits back down and the piano is struck up and Mr. Fringe Martin is starting to sing 'Joy to the World' from the beginning again when Crazy Nathan gets up from the front pew and—"

Mrs. Madison interrupted him. "Now, now!" she said. "It's not a good spirit at Christmas, or any other season, to refer to Nathan Godfrey as Crazy Nathan. I know other boys and girls sometimes call him that, but I don't ever want to hear any of you do it."

"It's uncharitable," said Clara May, and D. J. asked, "Why? 'Cause he's your sweetheart?"

"That's unkind too," said Mrs. Madison. "It's wrong to make any sort of joke about Nathan."

"Anyhow," said Renfroe, "Charlie Brand is Clara May's sweetheart."

"Aw, I know it!" said D. J. "I was just, oh, I don't know," he added, shrugging.

"You were being *uncharitable*," said Renfroe, glad to have a chance to use one of Clara May's words right off. Everybody laughed—including Renfroe, as if he hadn't been the one to speak of Nathan Godfrey as Crazy Nathan.

Nathan was fifteen years old and he was retarded. He didn't go to school, but his family always brought him to church. He would sit in the front pew, staring straight ahead, and the only time he had ever left his place, except when led to or from it by his younger sister, Opal Ann, was at last year's Christmas program. Then he had stood up, after everyone else had sat down, and walked up to see where the hay had caught fire. Opal Ann had hurried to his side and taken him by the hand and led him back to his seat.

D. J. refilled the corn popper and shook it over hot coals while Mr. Madison told them Nathan was being sent to a special school for the handicapped after the holidays. It was in the mountains, he said, and the Civic Club in town was going to pay for the boy to go there. "But about your imitation, Renfroe," he said, "I don't know that anybody at church would care to be reminded of all the things that went wrong at last year's pageant. So why don't you think of something else?" Then he laughed. "And maybe it's uncharitable of me, but as clever as you are at doing imitations, I don't personally think you could sound as awful as Fringe Martin!"

At that, Renfroe, D. J., and Clara May all three began

singing "Joy to the World" as loud and as off key as they possibly could. Renfroe guessed it was all right to do it because he saw his mother smiling. Anyway, Mr. Fringe Martin wasn't retarded; he just couldn't sing.

The next afternoon, out in the back yard, Renfroe tried again to think of what he could do at the party. Mrs. Gibbons wanted something everybody, even small children, might enjoy. That was what she had said. He thought and thought . . . and had almost given up on a new imitation when an idea came to him. He believed it would be just right, and it had come to him so suddenly he almost felt that someone had whispered it to him. He looked around, but nobody was there. Then he noticed the angel on the smokehouse door. She was looking straight at him.

A Rope
of His Own

On Christmas morning Renfroe found three gifts under the tree for him. One was a plow-line, except that to him it was a lasso. He had wished for the longest kind of time for a rope of his own, and now he had it.

His second gift was a Yo-yo. The string was too long, and D. J., who had also received one, suggested he cut it off. But Renfroe planned to grow taller as time went on, so he decided it would be better to stand on a chair to play with the Yo-yo now than to have a string that was too short for him later.

His third and nicest present was a pocket watch. It was a Mickey Mouse one, with a picture of Mickey himself on it, looking just as pert as he did in the funny papers. One of his arms, stretched out, was the minute hand, and his other arm, bent at the elbow, was the hour hand. There was also a small hand at the bottom for keeping track of the seconds. It was fun to watch it spin around as if it didn't have a second to lose.

Renfroe had never dreamed of owning anything as wonderful as the watch. He sat and looked at it till he was called to breakfast, and during the meal he checked to see what time it was after almost every bite. When breakfast was finished he went back to the front room and sat near the Christmas tree, holding his watch in front of him. Occasionally he would stand on a chair or the bench by the fireplace and try his Yo-yo. But he couldn't get it to climb back up the string more than one time out of every three or four tries.

When the sun had been up long enough to melt the frost, he went outside to play. He stood on a chicken coop and tried his Yo-yo from there, but his luck was no better than it had been inside. So he put the Yo-yo in his pocket and walked out to the wagon shelter. He showed his watch to Andrew Jackson, who was curled up on a pile of burlap bags in the corner, but the dog only thumped his tail once against the ground and closed his eyes. "Don't you have any Christmas spirit?" asked Renfroe, and Andrew Jackson thumped his tail another time but did not look up. Renfroe went back into the house to see if anybody there cared to know what time it was.

"I was hoping somebody would come along and give me the correct time," said his father. He was sitting on the wood box near the stove while Mrs. Madison spooned broth over a chicken that was roasting on its back in the oven.

"Well," said Renfroe, studying Mickey Mouse, "if you wouldn't mind waiting four more minutes it'll be ten o'clock."

"I guess I have time to wait," Mr. Madison teased, "this being a holiday and all."

Renfroe sat down in the rocking chair near the window, holding the watch in a good light. "Now it's three minutes till ten o'clock," he said, and a minute later he announced that there were only two minutes to go. Next came the one-minute-till signal, and when that minute was up he hopped out of his chair. "Ten o'clock exactly!" he said happily.

Then he asked if he could go through the woods to see if the Claytons had moved yet. The Claytons were a family who had lived in the house at the edge of the woods since early fall. The father worked for the sawmill, but it had closed down a month ago, and they were to move again. Mrs. Madison said it was all right for Renfroe to go, but for him to button up his jacket and to pull the flaps of his cap down over his ears. An earache, she reminded him, might keep him home from the pageant and party at the church tonight. She also told him not to stay too long.

On the way through the woods Renfroe played with his rope. D. J. had tied a loop in it for him, and as he ran along the path he pretended he was a cowboy with a lasso. Whenever he saw a tree stump it became a steer or a wild horse, and he would rope it—or try to. Usually he missed, but every now and then he roped a target. By the time he came out of the woods his aim had improved a bit over what it had been.

All the children in the Clayton family were girls, and they were at the woodpile, playing dolls with sticks of

stovewood, when Renfroe arrived. Clarrie was Renfroe's age, Mary Martha was older, and Little Lucy was the youngest.

"Good morning, Renfroe," said Clarrie, smiling at him, and Mary Martha asked, "Where'd you get that rope?"

"Santa Claus brought it to me," he answered. "What did he bring you?"

"A diamond ring and a velvet dress," said Mary Martha, "plus a few other things that are none of your business."

"Aw, Mary Martha! How come you make up lise?" said Clarrie. To Renfroe she said, "She got the same as the rest of us, that's what she got."

"You don't know!" said Mary Martha. "I might have hid my presents before you saw them."

"I got an orange and an apple and a candy bar," said Little Lucy.

"Is that all?" asked Renfroe. "Why, that wasn't hardly worth hanging up your stocking for, was it?"

"Oh, yes," said Little Lucy. "The candy and orange were real good, and I'm saving the apple till tomorrow."

Clarrie said pleasantly, "It was nice of Santa Claus to leave you that jump rope, Renfroe."

"It's not a jump rope, it's a lasso," said Renfroe. "And besides it, I got a Yo-yo—and this!" He took the watch from his pocket, and all three girls gathered in closer to look at it.

"It's beautiful," said Clarrie, and Little Lucy asked,

"Reckon the same Santa Claus came to your house that came to ours?"

Mary Martha changed the subject. She said, "Let us play with your jump rope, Renfroe."

"It's not a jump rope. It's a lasso."

"Then let us play jump rope with your lasso."

Renfroe agreed, and he turned the rope at one end while Little Lucy held it at the other. Clarrie and Mary Martha did the jumping, and they were good at it. They chanted verses in time to their jumping, and when they had warmed up, they would call out "Hot peas!" That was the signal for the rope to be turned as fast as possible. Now they jumped to one of their favorite verses:

> Papa in a tail coat,
>   Mamma in a gown,
> Chicken in the hot stove
>   Upside down.
>
> Cake is on the inside,
>   Icing on the out,
> Coffee in the coffeepot
>   Spewing from the spout.
>
> Ham is in the skillet,
>   Eggs are in the cheese,
> Now all we need for supper
>   Is GOOD HOT PEAS!

At that, the rope turned faster and faster, and everyone began counting. The number of times the rope was jumped was supposed to be the number of peas that would be eaten for supper. Renfroe began to get hungry thinking about it, and said he should be going.

"Don't leave!" said Clarrie.

"It's time to eat," said Renfroe. Remembering the verse the girls had chanted, he told them, "We've got a chicken cooking in the stove upside down."

"Is your papa in a tail coat and your mamma in a gown?" asked Little Lucy.

Mary Martha spoke up. "We're not having chicken today," she said, strutting around the chopping block to where she had been playing when Renfroe arrived. "We decided to have fried steak and turkey and pork chops and ice cream and chocolate pie instead."

"Mary Martha!" said Clarrie. "How come you make up such whopping tales? You know plain as I do that we're having biscuits and gravy and middling meat."

"And syrup," added Little Lucy.

Renfroe almost said it didn't sound like much of a Christmas dinner to him, but he guessed that would not be wise. Maybe Mary Martha liked pretending she would have all those good things to eat, the way all three girls pretended that the sticks of stovewood they had tied scraps of cloth around were dolls and the little pieces of kindling, with rags around them, were the babies.

"If you go," Little Lucy said, "we won't have a rope to play with." But Renfroe said he had to leave anyway.

On his way home he did not use the rope as a lasso. He wasn't in a mood to play, maybe because he kept thinking about what it would have been like to have received only an apple and an orange and a candy bar from Santa Claus. His own family was not well off, he knew, and there had been times when he almost wished he were one of those boys in storybooks who got things like real ponies for Christmas. But that was before he had gotten the watch. He knew he wouldn't trade it for a whole drove of ponies. He also knew now that his family was rich compared to some others, and he guessed he was lucky to be who he was.

Suddenly it came to him that he could have lent his rope to the girls. Then it struck him that he could even have given it to them, but he tried to put that out of his mind. Him, give away his rope? Well, he admitted, he could have gone back to borrowing one from a harness peg, but that wasn't the same as having one of his own. Still, Clarrie, Mary Martha, and Little Lucy had nothing to play with except those sticks of wood.

He thought about it until he got to the back yard. By then he was telling himself that he had been generous enough in sharing the rope. Yes, he said firmly, that was enough. Just then he happened to glance at the smokehouse door, but the angel did not appear even to notice him. She was looking out over his head as if she might never look down at him again.

Galloping
Hoofs

The Madisons ate their Christmas dinner in the middle of the day. Besides the baked chicken, there were candied sweet potatoes, biscuits and giblet gravy, applesauce, and for dessert a pecan pie. After the pie Renfroe decided to try out his imitation, the one he would perform at the church that night.

"I think I'll do it before I tell you what it is," he said.

"Well, that's a change!" said D. J.

"Here it is," said Renfroe. "An imitation. By Renfroe Madison." And he began by making a galloping noise. Then he made a noise that sounded like a horse neighing, followed by a rattling kind of sound, like wood crackling in a hot fire. Next came a *swoosh*, and that was all. "Now can you guess what it was?" he asked.

"I can," said D. J. "It was a herd of wild horses."

Clara May asked, "What about the rattling noise?"

"That could have been a skeleton chasing them down the road," said D. J., who had been reading scary stories lately. "With his dry bones clicking against each other, the skeleton alarmed the horses so much that they ran smack over a cliff. The *swoosh* was them falling through the air."

"No, that wasn't it," said Renfroe.

"Of course it wasn't!" said Mr. Madison. "I knew right off that it was only our mules, who had somehow gotten out of the barn in the middle of the night, galloping by the house. And the rattling noise, well, that was rain falling on our tin roof at the same time, and the *swoosh* was me pulling the bedcovers up over my head so I could go back to sleep on account of I wouldn't be able to see to catch them till daybreak anyhow."

Everybody laughed, and Renfroe said, "No, that wasn't it either. But you're closer to it than D. J. was."

Mrs. Madison said, "Since it's for the Christmas party I'd say the neighing was not made by wild horses nor mules, but by a donkey: the one from the Bible, carrying the Virgin Mary and being led by Joseph into the city of Bethlehem to look for a place to stay. The crackling noise might have meant that they came onto cobblestone streets. Wouldn't hoofbeats on cobblestones make a nice crisp sound?"

"They might," agreed Mr. Madison, "but what was the *swoosh?*"

"It could have been someone rushing past," said Mrs. Madison. "After all, Bethlehem was crowded with people at that particular time. That's why there was no room at the inn for the Holy Family."

"That would have been a good imitation," said Renfroe, "but that's not what it was."

"I'll bet I can guess," said Clara May.

"I'll bet you can too," agreed Renfroe. Sometimes he felt that she could tell just exactly what he was thinking.

"Well," she said, "the galloping and the neighing were not done by horses or mules or a donkey, but by reindeer."

"You've figured it out!" said Renfroe.

D. J. spoke up. "I don't think reindeer make a neighing noise."

"Renfroe's reindeer might," said Clara May.

"Well, yeah," admitted D. J. "Renfroe's reindeer might cackle as far as that goes."

"So I guessed it!" said Clara May. "The reindeer galloped to a halt on our roof, and the *swoosh* was Santa Claus jumping down the chimney."

"And where does the rattling noise fit in?" asked Mr. Madison. He smiled, and so did Renfroe—thinking Clara May would guess that part too.

Clara May laughed. "That's easy," she said. "That was only the clatter of small hoofs. The reindeer's babies had come tagging along behind the sleigh."

"I should have known!" said Mr. Madison.

"But that's not it," said Renfroe, shaking his head. Mr. Madison guessed then that it was the crackle of a good fire, even if it was a mean trick on Santa Claus to make him land in a roaring blaze, but Renfroe said that wasn't it either. Everybody kept guessing until at last the whole family gave up on what the rattling noise had been. Renfroe explained to them, "It was snow."

"Snow!" said D. J. and Mr. Madison at the same time.

"Snow falling on our tin roof," said Renfroe. "That's why you were close, Pa, when you guessed about the rain."

"Sounded more like a hailstorm," said D. J., and Mrs. Madison told Renfroe snow didn't make any noise, that it fell softly without the least sound.

Renfroe had never seen snow, and he was envious of D. J. and Clara May because they both remembered two good storms. In the section of Georgia where the Madisons lived, south of Atlanta but still in the northern half of the state, there was snow some winters, but not every year. And it just hadn't worked out that even one flake of it had fallen since Renfroe had been big enough to remember. People kept telling him that sooner or later it would snow again, but he wondered if it ever would.

Nutty
and the Yo-yo

What'd you get for Christmas?"
asked Renfroe, out trying to lasso a washpot when Nutty
came over in the afternoon.

"Not anything yet," said Nutty.

"*Yet!*" said Renfroe. "Why, Christmas is nearly over."

"I know," said Nutty. "Granny and Grandpa ordered
me some new clothes, but the package hasn't come."

"Didn't they give you anything to play with?"

"They didn't feel up to going into town the way they'd
planned," said Nutty. "But it's all right. They're feeling
better today, and that's nicer than a Christmas gift."

"Too bad they didn't get better yesterday," said Renfroe, "while the stores were still open." Then he showed
off his main present. "It's a real fine watch," he said.

Nutty teased him. "You'll be expecting me to believe
it keeps time!"

"Of course it does!" answered Renfroe. "You can even
see it keeping time. That little bitty hand going around

down there at the bottom ticks off every single second." Nutty was looking at it when D. J. came out of the house.

"Check this!" said D. J., spinning his Yo-yo out to one side. Then he flung it straight toward the ground and let it spin around—"idlying," as he called it. "Now come back!" he said, as if he were talking to the Yo-yo, and the Yo-yo climbed back up the string as if it had heard.

"Say!" said Nutty. "You're almost as good as Spider Jones."

"Better, I expect!" said D. J., laughing. Spider Jones, Renfroe knew, was one of their friends at school who was noted for being able to do dazzling things with a Yo-yo.

"I think I'll practice with mine," said Renfroe, taking his own Yo-yo out of his pocket.

"You mean you've got one too?" said Nutty. "And, say, it's a good one like D. J.'s! Maybe that was what Grandpa was planning to buy me if he had gone into town."

"I can Yo-yo from the top step," said Renfroe.

"Why not from here?"

"The string's too long."

D. J. spoke up. "He won't cut it off on account of he says he'll grow to it. And you know Renfroe, with a mind of his own!"

"Well, I will grow to it!" said Renfroe, climbing the steps.

Standing at the end of the top one, he threw out the Yo-yo. He spun it down with real flair, but somehow he didn't manage to yank the string at just the right time, and the Yo-yo stayed at the bottom, dangling crazily. He

rewound it, tried again but missed, and finally, on the third try, got it to climb back up the string twice before it played out. "You can have a turn with it," he told Nutty.

"Thank you," said Nutty, accepting the Yo-yo. He spun it down and up, down and up, smoothly, but could not make it spin around at the bottom, "idlying," the way D. J. could. D. J. said the end of the string that was attached to it should be split and tied with a special knot, and Renfroe asked for his to be tied in this way too. It was not until after D. J. had done it that he said it would also make the regular kind of spinning more difficult than ever. But he promised to tie the string back the way it had been if Renfroe would let Nutty practice with it first.

"Oh, all right," said Renfroe, going across the yard to play with his lasso again. He tried roping a rooster but it ran away, and he used an empty nail keg as his target next.

In midafternoon Mrs. Madison called all three boys into the house to get warm. While they were there Mr. Madison, standing in front of the open fire, took a turn with D. J.'s Yo-yo while Clara May passed around a box of chocolate-covered cherries Charlie Brand had given her for Christmas.

Mrs. Madison stood at the window, looking out. "The sky's awfully gray," she said. "I hope it's not going to rain before the program tonight."

"Those don't look like rain clouds," said D. J., and Mr. Madison said he thought it was too cold for rain anyway.

The boys returned to the yard when they were warmed through and played a while longer. When Clara May came out with the milking pails, they knew it was time for the afternoon chores, and D. J. went to the pasture to catch Twilight and Effie. He would bring them to the wagon shelter and hitch them to the two-horse wagon that would take the family to the church after supper.

Nutty said he must go home and see about his work too, but he stayed in the yard with Renfroe for a few more minutes, spinning the Yo-yo out at a new angle. Then he said, "I guess I'd better be off," as if he wished he didn't have to leave, "but I sure am much obliged to you for the use of your Yo-yo." He handed it back to Renfroe and headed toward the road.

Renfroe watched him walk away, wondering if maybe he should have told him to take the Yo-yo home and give it back at the church tonight—or maybe keep it till to-morrow. Then something seemed to tell him that he should have given the Yo-yo to Nutty for keeps. But why should he have done that? Didn't Nutty's grandparents have enough money to live in a bit more comfort than most of the people hereabouts? His grandpa was a retired railroad man and would probably get around to buying all sorts of things later. But a voice inside Renfroe's head spoke up: "Yes, but it doesn't matter how much Nutty gets then; he doesn't have anything special today, and he liked the Yo-yo, and you really aren't having much fun with it, are you?" His answer to this was: "Still, I didn't get that awfully much."

"Why, you got the watch!" the voice came back at him. "And the Yo-yo might have made Nutty happier than something big his grandpa buys for him."

Renfroe thought of running to catch up with Nutty, but he didn't. He said to himself, "Of course, if I were a rich boy and Santa Claus had brought me two or three bicycles and a carload of firecrackers and a bushel basket full of chocolate-covered cherries and a big storybook with colored pictures, why, I'd probably give Nutty one of the bicycles and as many firecrackers and chocolate-covered cherries as he'd care to tote home!" It made him feel better, thinking how generous he would be if he had all those things, and he started toward the barn to see if Clara May wanted to sing to the cows.

Crossing the yard, he looked toward the angel on the smokehouse door, imagining she was pleased at how generous he would be if he were a rich boy. She would understand, he felt certain, but when he looked at her he saw that she had turned away. It was only that the wind had twisted her around slightly, but it looked to Renfroe as if she had turned her back to him on purpose.

The Story
Acted Out

Mr. Fringe Martin read the Christmas story at the pageant. Maybe this was to keep him from singing, thought Renfroe as the program got under way. He read a few lines and then stopped when he finished a verse from the Bible about "the city of David, which is called Bethlehem," and a group of ladies sitting behind the piano sang "O Little Town of Bethlehem."

All the lamps in the church had been turned off except one in the far corner, and it was turned only high enough for Miss Lettie Redding to see to play the piano and for Mr. Martin to do his reading. But Mr. Otis Conway had a big stand-up flashlight, which he was using as a spotlight for the program. He flashed it onto whatever part of the stage needed to be lighted at any one time. Then he would turn it off and the stage would be nearly dark while the players got set for whatever was next.

The light was flashed onto the middle of the stage when Mr. Martin read about Joseph and Mary looking for a

place to stay, and the audience saw Clara May and her friend Charlie Brand draped in robes and acting as if they were knocking at the door of an inn. The light was soon taken off them, and the story moved along to the part about the three Wise Men.

49

Monroe Castor, Buck Jordan, Jr., and Nutty were the Wise Men. Monroe was the only one with a line to speak, and he said it nice and clear. It was about plans to follow a star that was shining overhead to see what it was all about, and as soon as he had said it the ladies sang "There's a Song in the Air, There's a Star in the Sky."

Next, Mr. Martin read of shepherds who were abiding in the field, keeping watch over their flock by night, but he must have come to that part sooner than Britt Castor and D. J. thought he would. They were the shepherds, and when the light was flashed onto them they were having a game of poking at each other in the dark with the long crooked-handled canes that were part of their costumes. They stopped at once and stood up straight, but Renfroe wondered if anybody would think "abiding in the field" meant swatting at each other with long sticks. That's probably what Nathan Godfrey would think—if Nathan, sitting in the front pew, could think at all.

The next part of the program was what Renfroe was anxious to see, and it was not easy waiting for it. If "abiding" meant waiting patiently, as he had been told it did, then he was not doing a very good job of abiding in his seat, because D. J. had told him what was going to happen: Mr. Speed Ellison had rigged up a well pulley to an overhead beam, and according to D. J., anybody who wasn't too heavy could be drawn up and down, from the floor to the ceiling, like a bucket of water. The plan had been for one of the younger girls of the church to be the herald angel in the Christmas story. She was to be lifted to the ceiling just before her part in the program and then come slowly drifting down when the light was on her. But the only girl daring enough to get into the harness and appear to be flying down to earth had not been able to remember what she was to say once she got there. Hoot Castor had been called on to take her place.

Sure enough, while the light was on D. J. and Britt, the angel appeared, and if Renfroe hadn't known about the well pulley he would have sworn Hoot came down from out of the sky. Lace curtains had been tied around his overalls, and he was flapping cardboard wings as if he really were flying. When his feet touched the floor he stopped flapping the wings and said, "Behold, I bring you good tidings of great joy," and then he told the shepherds they would find Jesus wrapped in swaddling clothes, lying in a manger.

At that, the ladies sang one verse each of "It Came upon a Midnight Clear" and "Away in a Manger." When the songs ended, D. J. and Britt pretended to be going off in search of the Christ Child while Hoot, the herald angel, was lifted back into the air.

The last scene of all showed Joseph and Mary at the manger, with the Wise Men kneeling off to one side and the shepherds at the other, while everybody in the church sang "Silent Night." Then a prayer was said, and the program was finished.

Renfroe hoped the grownups had liked it enough to keep letting young people act out the Christmas story. Maybe next year, or the next, he could be in it. From what he heard while the pews were being pushed aside for the party he guessed everybody was pleased. Mrs. Mel Redgrave called it "impressive" and Miss Alice Flinn said it was the most "inspiring" pageant she had ever in her life seen, except maybe the one in Charlotte, North Carolina, that time she had visited a cousin up there.

Renfroe would remember to tell those words to Clara May—"impressive" and "inspiring"—in case she ever wanted to use them, but just now it was time for the party to begin.

Crazy Nathan

First there was a poem, "A Pig Ate the Christmas Tree," by Mrs. Freddy Whitt. She had made it up herself. Then there was a song that didn't have any words to it, played by Miss Lettie Redding at the piano and Mr. Carl Royal on a homemade banjo. The banjo was made of wires stretched across a cigar box that had been nailed to a broom handle. Then Chester Castor performed a number on a row of bottles. A different amount of water was in each of the bottles, and Chester picked out a lively tune by tapping them with a short stick.

Next, Renfroe did his imitation, telling first that it was to be Santa Claus landing on a roof to deliver presents. Instead of the rattling noise, he threw in a "Ho! Ho! Ho!" and everybody said afterward that he sure could do a good belly laugh for someone as little as he was.

Then refreshments were served, and people began moving around. Grown persons talked with each other, and younger ones gathered with friends their own age and compared Christmas gifts. Everyone was laughing and talking—all except Nathan Godfrey. He sat on a bench and stared in front of him.

His sister, Opal Ann, took him a bowl of ambrosia. Opal Ann was only a year and a half older than Renfroe, but she looked like a little old lady. She coaxed Nathan to eat the ambrosia by offering him a spoonful at a time. Renfroe, remembering his father had said that fifteen-year-old Nathan was to be sent to a special school in the mountains, went over to where they sat. "I hear Nathan's going to be sent off," he said.

"Yes," answered Opal Ann pleasantly. "And he's real happy about going to that . . . institution." She said "institution" the way Renfroe said words he learned from Clara May when he wasn't certain he was using them right. Opal Ann continued, "I sure will miss him at home, but he's going to learn all sorts of useful things where he's going. Aren't you, Nathan?"

She looked at her brother, who sat staring straight ahead. He said nothing, but Renfroe asked, "What sort of useful things?"

"I don't know exactly," said Opal Ann, "but we've heard they've got experts who can teach people like him how to do some things for themselves."

It occurred to Renfroe that Opal Ann and her brother were likely the only people in the church who had not seen his Mickey Mouse watch. Maybe it would be nice to show it to them. "Do you think Nathan would care to see my watch?" he asked, taking it from his pocket.

"Why, that's a lovely timepiece!" said Opal Ann.

"Yes, it is," agreed Renfroe. "It's the finest thing I've ever owned by myself."

Opal Ann added, "My, isn't it beautiful, Nathan?"

Nathan said nothing, but he did reach out for the watch and Renfroe let him hold it. He noticed how the older boy studied it. Perhaps the second hand, going round and round, was what he liked. It was the first time Renfroe had ever seen him appear to be looking at any one thing. Usually he had an empty stare that didn't seem to focus on anything. After he had looked at the watch for a long time, Nathan did something else Renfroe had never seen him do: He smiled.

"I didn't know he knew how to smile," said Renfroe.

"Of course he knows how," said Opal Ann, but she admitted he didn't smile often. "Now give the watch back," she said to Nathan. "And we must thank Renfroe for sharing his nice present with us."

Nathan didn't say thank you, but he did hand the watch back. Maybe he could be "trained" after all, thought Renfroe, even if he was fifteen already and had to be fed by someone.

D. J., over by the front door with Doris Castor, motioned that it was time to go home, and Renfroe started toward the coat rack. He saw that his mother and father were putting on their wraps. Halfway there an idea came to him and he stopped. He took a few more steps, then stopped again. He stood still, thinking, and then turned

and went back to where Opal Ann was eating her bowl of ambrosia. "I've decided to give Nathan my watch," he said, holding out his Christmas gift.

Opal Ann looked at him for a moment without saying anything—as if she could not believe what she had heard. At last she spoke. "Why, we wouldn't think of letting you give it up!" she said, just as Nathan reached out and took the watch.

Renfroe said, "Maybe he will have more time at that . . . institution. . . to admire it than I will at school."

"But it's the finest thing you've ever owned," said Opal Ann. "You said so yourself, and you must keep it."

"No," said Renfroe firmly. "I want him to have it."

"Well, my!" said Opal Ann, looking at Nathan, who was smiling again as he studied the watch. "It's just too generous of you, it really is. Why, you must be the most unselfish person in the world! And we certainly do thank you, don't we, Nathan?"

Renfroe left without waiting for Nathan's answer, which he knew would not come, or for the comments Opal Ann would be making, as if Nathan really would have said thank you if only she had not kept talking.

Renfroe walked slowly, wondering if maybe he should turn around again. He could tell Opal Ann that he guessed she had been right, perhaps it would be best for Nathan to give back the present. But no, his mind was made up: He had given away the watch and that was that! He hurried to the coat rack, feeling better than he could ever remember. It was almost a miracle, it seemed to him, that he could have given away his favorite belonging and feel so good about it. But if that was a miracle, what happened next seemed even more like one.

"It's snowing!" said Mr. Madison, leading the way out into the night. He held up the lantern he carried, and Renfroe looked toward it. Big feathery flakes of snow filled the air. "It's snowing!" called Mr. Castor, who was untying his mules at the hitching rail, and someone across the yard called, "It's snowing!" Word spread inside the church, and soon everybody came outdoors.

Instead of a miracle, the grownups said it was a coincidence that it had begun to snow while everyone was in the church on Christmas night. But they were as pleased about it as the boys and girls. And Andrew Jackson, waiting in the wagon, got so excited that he stood up, looked around, and wagged his tail twice.

There seemed to be lanterns everywhere, and the falling snow softened the light given off by each of them. Renfroe knew for certain he had never seen anything more beautiful in his whole life. He didn't believe he could have said how he really felt even if he had known as many big words as Clara May, but he agreed with Mrs. Freddy Whitt that it was all just as pretty as a store-bought Christmas card.

Grownups called "Happy Holidays!" back and forth as the wagons were driving away, and children called to one another that they would get together in the morning to have snow battles and build snow men and eat snow ice cream.

Renfroe was happy all the way home, thinking about what the next day would be like. Of course, he thought of his watch too. Once he even reached into his pocket for it, forgetting he had given it away.

But he believed he had done the right thing. He was telling himself that yes, he *had* done the right thing, just as his father drove the wagon into the back yard. A ray of light from the lamp by the driver's seat fell briefly across the angel on the smokehouse door, and he saw that she was looking at him. Then she was caught, just as briefly, by light from the lantern on the tail gate. At that moment she waved at Renfroe. He knew it was only that a gentle breeze had lifted her arm into the air, but he waved back anyway.

ABOUT THE AUTHOR

ROBERT BURCH *was born in Fayette County, Georgia, where he grew up with seven brothers and sisters. Upon graduating from high school during World War II he went into the Army and served in New Guinea and Australia. When the war was over he traveled extensively. He worked for a while in Japan, and then, on a Danish freighter, visited many ports in the Orient, North Africa, and Europe. Afterward he spent eight years in New York City but he has now moved back to Georgia.*

His books include Tyler, Wilkin, and Skee, *the story of a year in the life of three brothers growing up on a farm;* D. J.'s Worst Enemy, *in which the central character of* Renfroe's Christmas *first appeared;* Skinny; Queenie Peavy; *and a picture book,* A Funny Place to Live.